MELISSA'S
STORY
Living with HIV

Created by
Andy Glynne and
Salvador Maldonado

W
FRANKLIN WATTS
LONDON • SYDNEY

Franklin Watts
First published in Great Britain in 2017 by The Watts Publishing Group

Mosaic Films, Shacklewell Lane, London E8 2EZ

Created by Andy Glynne and Salvador Maldonado

Editor: Sarah Silver

We would like to thank the Body & Soul charity for their advice on this subject.

ISBN 978 1 4451 5664 4

Printed in China

FSC
www.fsc.org

MIX
Paper from
responsible sources
FSC® C104740

Franklin Watts
An imprint of
Hachette Children's Group
Part of The Watts Publishing Group
Carmelite House
50 Victoria Embankment
London EC4Y 0DZ

An Hachette UK Company
www.hachette.co.uk
www.franklinwatts.co.uk

My name is Melissa
and I am HIV positive.

I'm the middle child in my family. Growing up
it was just my mum, we didn't have a dad around.
But I could always talk to my older sister and brother.

I felt really happy as a child.

I was told that I was HIV positive
when I was eleven.

My mum, the doctor and my older sister were there.

All I can remember thinking is,
'My life is over, I'm going to die.'

The doctor said I wouldn't die,
but that I had to take MEDICATION from that point on,
every day, for the rest of my life.

We all have an immune system
that keeps us HEALTHY and alive.
It fights off colds and other viruses.

HIV is like an ATTACKER of the immune system.
It comes in and battles with the things that are trying
to make you healthy. It's like a BATTLE between
the good, and the bad. And HIV is the bad.

If I take my medication, I'm helping my immune system.

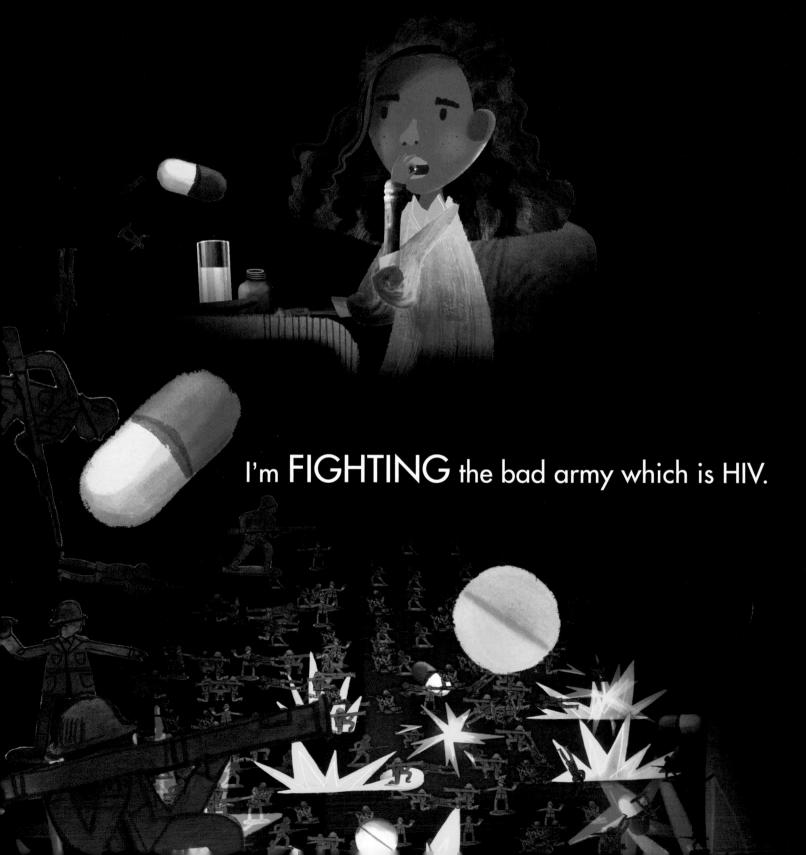

I'm **FIGHTING** the bad army which is HIV.

AIDS is the result of NOT TAKING your medication and managing your HIV. Having AIDS means your body has lost the power to fight the viruses and infections that attack you.

The doctor explained that there are different ways of getting HIV.

One way is through breastfeeding, from the mother to the child. I assumed that I got HIV from my mum.

I thought that I couldn't tell people about HIV ...

... because my mum wasn't able to tell me.

So inside I always felt like I was keeping a SECRET.

I sometimes felt like I was WEARING A MASK
and playing a character.

I'd put on this face and be BRAVE and happy and smiley. But inside I was actually feeling very SMALL. It was like a weight I was carrying around all the time.

I thought if I told my friends, they wouldn't understand.

Taking my medication makes me feel sick.
I never eat breakfast because it makes me throw up.

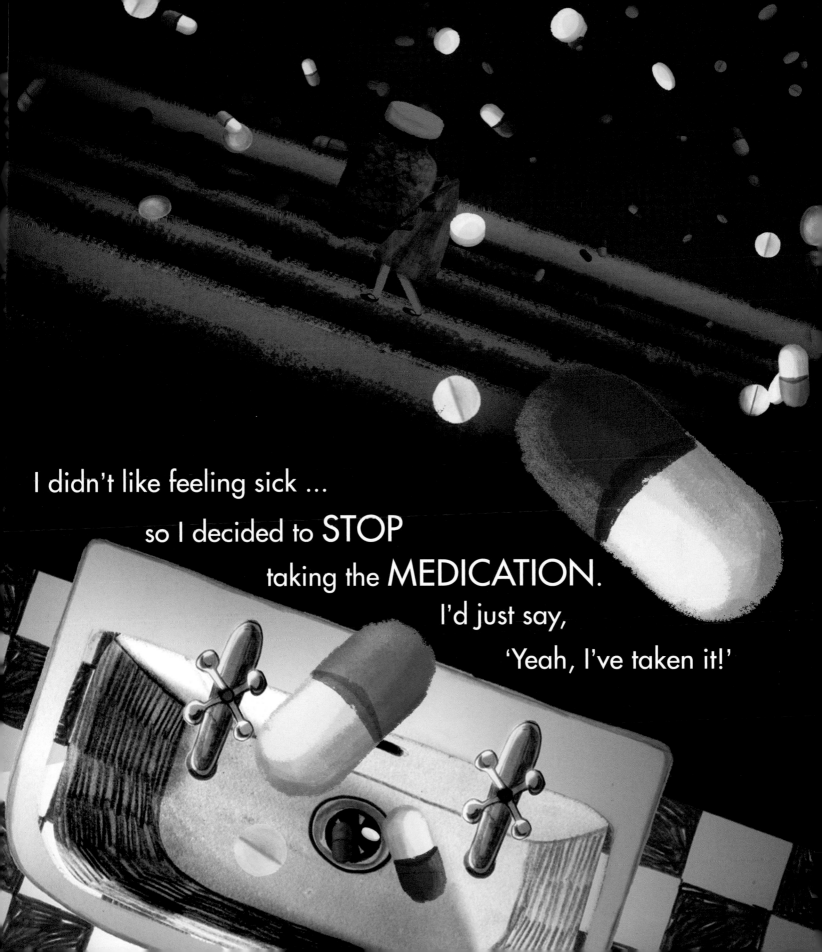

I didn't like feeling sick ...
so I decided to STOP
taking the MEDICATION.
I'd just say,
'Yeah, I've taken it!'

Then one day I was sitting down in class
and I couldn't get up!
My legs were really hurting me.

I had to go to the HOSPITAL.

They said that it was arthritis in my leg
and they had to OPERATE on my knees.

Because I wasn't taking my medication, my immune system was breaking down. I was getting weaker but I didn't feel it until that happened.

After the operation I went to a place where
I could **MEET** other people who were HIV positive.

That made me feel so much more
comfortable in my skin because I knew
that I WASN'T ALONE. It gave me confidence.

When I moved up to secondary school
I told two of my friends that I am HIV positive.

At first they didn't believe me
because I just tell too many jokes!

Then I showed them my medication
and they said 'Wow! This is REAL!'

Then they said, 'Okay, but you're still you!'
That made me feel a lot more CONFIDENT
about what I was dealing with. I know I will
always have to take medication, but I will also
always have friends to SUPPORT me.

FURTHER INFORMATION ABOUT HIV

Our immune system defends us against invading germs, such as bacteria and viruses. HIV stands for Human Immunodeficiency Virus. It is a virus that attacks the immune system itself, making it weak. With medication, someone with HIV can lead a happy and productive life. If left untreated, HIV can result in many different health issues and may develop into AIDS.

How do you get HIV?
HIV is transmitted from one person to another through bodily fluids such as blood, breast milk, semen and vaginal fluids. Children who are HIV positive have usually been passed the virus by their mother during pregnancy, childbirth or through breast milk. When doctors discover that a child is HIV positive, the child is likely to start taking medication that will control the virus and support the child's immune system. If the child does not take the pills regularly, they can develop health problems like Melissa did.

What is AIDS?
If someone who is HIV positive does not receive treatment or does not take their pills properly, they can develop AIDS. AIDS stands for Acquired Immune Deficiency Syndrome and it is the most advanced stage of the HIV infection. The immune system of someone with AIDS is no longer able to fight infections and so they will develop serious diseases such as cancer, pneumonia or tuberculosis. The earlier someone is treated for HIV, the less likely it is that they will ever develop AIDS.

Living with HIV
Children who are HIV positive, like Melissa, can feel very alone and frightened. Other children may not understand how HIV is passed on. HIV is NOT passed on by kissing or hugging, or by sharing cutlery, a toilet seat, a bath or a swimming pool. It is important for *everyone* to understand how HIV works and how it can affect people. This is particularly important when young people become sexually active – it is everybody's responsibility to take care of themselves and those around them.

For more information and support visit the Body & Soul charity website:
www.bodyandsoulcharity.org

The complete Living with... series.
Real-life testimonies of children living with illness.

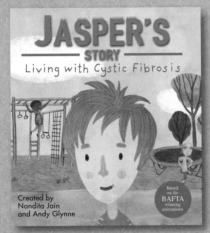

JASPER'S STORY
Living with Cystic Fibrosis

Created by Nandita Jain and Andy Glynne

Based on the BAFTA winning animations

978 14451 5604 0

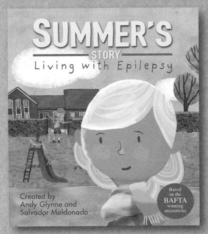

SUMMER'S STORY
Living with Epilepsy

Created by Andy Glynne and Salvador Maldonado

Based on the BAFTA winning animations

978 14451 5666 8

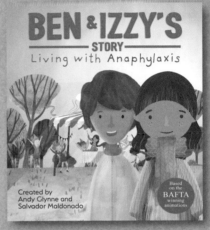

BEN & IZZY'S STORY
Living with Anaphylaxis

Created by Andy Glynne and Salvador Maldonado

Based on the BAFTA winning animations

978 14451 5662 0

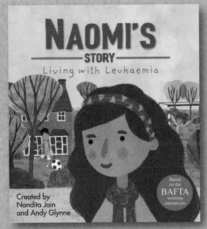

NAOMI'S STORY
Living with Leukaemia

Created by Nandita Jain and Andy Glynne

Based on the BAFTA winning animations

978 14451 5668 2

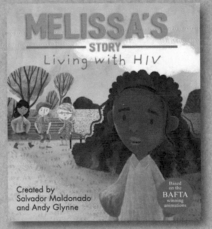

MELISSA'S STORY
Living with HIV

Created by Salvador Maldonado and Andy Glynne

Based on the BAFTA winning animations

978 14451 5664 4

FRANKLIN WATTS

www.franklinwatts.co.uk